MW01265125

CRAWL INTO THE NIGHT

CRAWL INTO THE NIGHT

A STORY ABOUT HUGH GLASS

To Jace —
I hope you enjoy my story —
Mrs. La Due

MARGIE LA DUE

ILLUSTRATED BY ANNE ELLINGSON

JOY IN THE MORNING PUBLISHING CO.
MUD BUTTE, SD

ISBN: 978-0-615-21459-7

CONTENTS

Dedication… … … … … … … … … … … … …13

Foreword… … … … … … … … … … … … …15

Grand River Grizzly … … … … … … … … …19

Left to Die … … … … … … … … … … … …25

Into the Night … … … … … … … … … … …31

The Crawl … … … … … … … … … … … …35

RESCUED! … … … … … … … … … … … …39

Ft. Kiowa at Last … … … … … … … … … …45

Historical Footnotes … … … … … … … … …49

About the Author … … … … … … … … … …53

About the Illustrator … … … … … … … … …54

Reflections of a First Time Author … … … … …55

Hugh Glass and the bear

MANY THANKS TO...

Phyllis Schmidt, Carol Taylor, Sue Wortmann and Jean Patrick...

your experience as authors, your wisdom and encouragement were invaluable...

Students at Bison School who kept asking me, "How's your book coming?"...

your interest fueled my desire to write...

Anne, who used to draw horses for me...

your illustrations make the story of Hugh Glass come alive.

DEDICATED TO...

All my former students; to my husband who tolerated my long hours at the computer; to my mom and dad who instilled in me a love of books; to Don Wilken, my 8th grade teacher; to my family and friends who supported and encouraged me; and to my Lord who blessed my efforts.

Hugh Glass Monument near Shadehill, SD

Reece Leonard standing in front of the Hugh Glass monument near Bison School, Bison, SD

FOREWORD

The story of Hugh Glass intrigued me since the 1960s when the author of "The Song of Hugh Glass," John Neihardt, visited Bison School. He was instrumental in the placement of two monuments that memorialize the 200-mile journey Hugh Glass made, much of it on his hands and knees. One monument sits in the Bison School parking lot. The other overlooks the spot where Glass was attacked by the grizzly at the forks of the Grand River, near present day Shadehill Reservoir.

Hugh Glass

Ashley Fur Company Makes Camp

*"Because of the Lord's great love
we are not consumed, for his compassions
never fail. They are new every morning;
great is your faithfulness."*
Lamentations 3:22-23

GRAND RIVER GRIZZLY

Beaver hats brought Major William Henry to the forks of the Grand River in Dakota Territory. He and the men with him were known as the Ashley Fur Company. They were headed to the Yellowstone River. There they planned to hunt beaver. Beaver hats were very popular headwear for men in 1823. Many, many hats could be made from the hundreds of beaver they hoped to find in the streams of the Yellowstone. These adventurers hoped to trap enough beaver to become rich men.

The hunters welcomed the Major's order to rest for the night. Their stomachs rumbled with hunger. They hadn't eaten since early that morning.

Hugh Glass, one of Henry's men, slid from his pony. "Better be for finding something for the frying pan. Be back with some fresh meat pronto," he called as he headed toward the river bottom.

A few days earlier, Arikara Indians (or Rees, as they were often called) had surprised the hunting party near the mouth of the Missouri. Some men had died in the battle. Hugh took an arrow in the leg while saving the life of his friend, Jim Bridger. Limping from his wound, Hugh disappeared into the bushes that lined the river bottoms. The late summer sun sinking in the western sky sent golden rays through the bushes.

Most of the men in the hunting party never went off alone. No one except the "old man" as Hugh was called.

Hugh Glass lost his family when he was just a youngster. They all died from the Black Plague, leaving him alone in the world. Then Hugh joined up with a ship's crew headed for the Gulf of Mexico only to find out when he was out to sea that he was sailing with pirates. He later escaped from the pirate ship, but was captured by a band of Pawnees. Hugh saved his own skin when he offered the Pawnee chief a gift of vermilion. This red powder was highly valued because it made excellent face paint. The chief was so impressed by the gift that he spared Hugh's life and they became close friends. The chief showed his admiration for Hugh by giving him a rifle, which Hugh called "Old Faithful", and he never let the gun out of his sight. Around the campfire, Hugh told the others of his escape from the Black Plague, pirates, and even Pawnee Indians. They all knew the old man could escape just about anything.

Hugh was deep into the bushes that lined the creek bottom. He was sure to find a deer or maybe an antelope nibbling on the ripe buffalo berries dangling from the branches.

"Maybe I'll jest grab some of these berries an' stop the rumblin' in my belly," Hugh muttered as he dropped his rifle, Ole Faithful, from his shoulder. He reached with both hands for the juicy prairie fruit.

Suddenly, from deep in the bushes, a grizzly stood on her hindquarters. Her towering height dwarfed Hugh. Her silver tipped fur glistened in the light of the sinking sun. By her side were two cubs. The quiet of the prairie evening was shattered as she roared her disapproval at Hugh's presence. She pawed angrily at empty air.

Grabbing Ole Faithful, Hugh aimed at the grizzly. She dropped on all fours, and charged. Hugh was an excellent sharpshooter and his first shot tore into her body. Stunned for a moment, she paused. Frantically, Hugh tried to reload but before he could get off another shot, the grizzly was on him. His coonskin cap went sailing as her claws ripped across his face and into his scalp. Blood gushed from Hugh's wounds, blinding him. The bear lifted him into the air. Ole Faithful fell into the nearby bushes.

Hugh Glass and the Grizzly

The grizzly held Hugh like a rag doll and then dropped him. His left leg twisted under him and he heard the bone snap. Before he could escape, the huge animal was on him, tearing at him with her 3-inch claws. Hugh struggled to pull his knife from his belt. With the last of his strength, he drove his knife deep into the grizzly.

Hearing the roars of the enraged grizzly and the blast from Hugh's gun, Major Henry and the other men raced toward the creek bottom. There they found Hugh, covered with blood. He appeared dead, as did the grizzly. Henry fired into the bear's body. With great effort, the men pulled the beast off the old man. Jim Bridger knelt, his ear to Hugh's heart. Filled with relief, his voice broke as he exclaimed, "The old man's not a goner yet!"

Bridger tenderly inspected the wounds to Hugh's battered body. Bringing water from the river, he washed and then wrapped the wounds with strips torn from clean shirts. "You poor old coon. That's the best I can do fer ya," Jim said as he knelt by his friend's limp and lifeless body.

The other men were busy skinning out the bear. The grizzly meat would provide many days of provisions. They salted and dried it. Once the bearskin was cleaned, they gently lifted Hugh onto the soft fur. Wrapped in bandages and unconscious, he appeared more dead than alive. As night fell, the men prepared to bed down. They knew they'd be burying Glass in the morning.

"Like a bear lying in wait…he dragged me from the path, mangled me, and left me without help."
Lamentations 3:10-11

LEFT TO DIE

For 2 days, they waited. Roving Ree Indians were a constant worry. The men were jumpy, and the time passed very slowly. Hugh hadn't moved or spoken. He hardly seemed to breathe. Jim stayed close by his side, wanting to be there if Hugh awakened.

On the 3rd night, Henry said they could wait no longer. They would head west taking the old man with them. A frame was constructed from branches. On this makeshift bed, they laid the bearskin. Then carefully Hugh's lifeless body was placed there with Old Faithful by his side.

At morning's first light, they broke camp and followed the river west. The men took turns carrying the old man. It was rough going and Hugh's groans increased with every step.

Major Henry soon called a halt near a grove of trees.

A nearby spring provided a refreshing drink. Resting, the men listened as the Major spoke. He explained that Hugh was slowing them down too much. His voice was quiet as he said, "I need two volunteers to stay behind and bury Glass when the time comes. There's money in it for you. As soon as he dies and you bury him, you can catch up to us or join us at the Yellowstone River."

With no hesitation, Jim Bridger stepped forward. "The old man saved my skin when we fought with them Rees. I'd a bin a goner if he hadn't a stayed with me. I reckon I should square that up with him. I'll stay behind and bury him. The money isn't why I'm doin' it. The old man's my friend. He'd do the same for me."

The men nervously looked at each other. They all wondered if the money was worth the risk. Staying behind could mean being captured or killed by the Rees. No one spoke for a long time. Finally, a man named Fitzgerald raised his hand. "I reckon I could stay behind with Jim to help bury the old coot, but only if ya pay me now."

Relieved to have volunteers, Major Henry quickly paid the two before they changed their minds. Now he and the others could continue west to the Yellowstone River. Fitz and Jim would stay behind and wait for Glass to die.

Dawn was in the eastern sky when Major Henry headed out with the others close behind. Fitz and Jim stood and watched until the hunting party disappeared in the distance. Alone now on the deserted prairie, the two sat down and waited.

Hours passed. Neither of them moved nor spoke as

they sat. Darkness came. They didn't dare start a campfire, for fear of being discovered by the Rees. The sounds of night surrounded them. An owl hooted, a distant coyote yipped at the rising moon.

Breaking the silence, Fitzgerald muttered, "I can't believe we agreed to such a fool hardy thing. We're plumb crazy to sit here and let the Rees finish us off too… let's high tail it out of here and ketch up with the others. That old coon, Glass, has one foot in the grave. We can tell the Major the old man died, cuz that's what he's gonna do anyhow…"

Jim tried not to hear those words. To show Fitz how he felt, he moved closer to his old friend. No, he couldn't leave Hugh to die alone. He'd never do that.

"Jim! Hey, Jim, are you listenin' to me, Jim?" Fitz persisted. He leaned toward Jim. "The old man is next to dead. If'n he could, he'd tell ya to save yerself. He sure doesn't want them Rees to find ya and kill ya after he saved yer skin! Yer way too young to die out here, Jim."

The long night dragged on. Hugh didn't move or even groan. For a long time Jim stared at him, hoping he would open his eyes or call out his name. Finally Jim mumbled, "Guess yer right. We need to get goin' and ketch up with the others befur the Rees git us. Old Hugh is gonna die and he won't know the difference if we don't stay to bury him."

Fitz, relieved to hear Jim agree with him, smiled a toothless grin in the dark. "Yep, Jim. Only you and me'll ever know that the old coot didn't git buried. It's the smart thing to do… to skee daddle 'fore we end up dead too!"

The men rolled up in their blankets and Fitz was soon snoring loudly. Jim lay awake for a long time and when he finally slept, he dreamed about Hugh saving his life back on the Missouri.

The next morning the two men prepared to break camp.

"Only a matter of hours, maybe a day, and the old man won't need nothing," Fitz said as he took Hugh's knife and his blanket. "Jest as well take his accoutrements. He ain't gonna need to build no fire now," Fitz growled. He reached over Hugh's still body to take the bag with his flint and steel. Then he picked up Ole Faithful. "Wouldn't want them Rees to find this fine rifle either."

Even though Hugh looked more dead than alive, he heard Fitz. He tried to cry out, "No! Don't take Ole Faithful. He struggled to reach out his hand and stop him. What did Fitz mean, he wouldn't need Old Faithful? Hugh never let Old Faithful out of his sight. Fitz had no right to take his rifle. Why didn't Jim stop him? Jim! Where was Jim?

Fitzgerald headed west without a backward glance, Hugh's rifle slung over his shoulder. Jim took one last look at his friend lying there as he spread the bearskin over Hugh's lifeless body. He whispered, "So long, old man," and he turned to follow Fitz.

Hugh tried desperately to call out. "No! Jim, don't go!" finally escaped his lips. Jim, hurrying to catch up with Fitz, didn't hear him.

Tears spilled from Hugh's eyes. Tears of anger at Fitz and Jim for leaving him alone. Tears of despair over the loss of Ole Faithful. How could he ever have called Jim his friend?

Left to die

"You have seen, O Lord, the wrong done to me."
Lamentations 3:59

INTO THE NIGHT

S everal days later, Hugh opened his eyes. Above him, billowy clouds floated in a clear blue sky. Birds twittered in nearby bushes. Flies buzzed around his blood-caked bandages. Hugh turned his head toward the sound of bubbling water. His parched throat longed for a drink. Gathering all his strength, he pushed back the bearskin and rolled toward the sound. Finally, he reached the spring. He laid his burning head into the coolness and drank.

He must eat to regain his strength. Some berries dangled from a nearby branch. He dragged his body near enough to grasp a few. Chewing was painful, so Hugh waited for the fruit to soften. Then he swallowed. Rolling back toward the bearskin, he quickly fell asleep, exhausted from his efforts. Grizzly bears, Fitz, Jim and Ole Faithful filled his dreams.

A wolf's howling awakened Hugh. A huge full moon

beamed down on him. Hugh wondered if the Rees had spotted him lying in the grove of trees. "Sooner or later, they'll find me," he muttered. The spring would also draw bears, coyotes, and wolves. Without a weapon, he'd not have a chance. To survive he had to get moving. And he must waste no time in getting started. Fall was upon the prairie. Winter would soon follow.

He rolled out of the hollow toward the spring and drank deeply. Then he laid his bandaged head in the water. The water eased the throbbing pain and cooled the fever that burned in his body.

Dragging his body back toward the hollow, he rested briefly. Then in the moonlight, he searched for buffalo berries. He stuffed several into his mouth and filled his pockets.

A plan was taking shape in Hugh's mind. "I'll head southeast. Foller the creek bottoms. Travel by night so the Rees won't spot me. Old sailor like me can keep my bearings by watching the stars. Got to get back to Ft. Kiowa. Once I get there I'll find Bridger and Fitz and make them pay for what they done…sneakin off with Ole Faithful! Leav'n me alone out here! I'll get even with those varmints, or I'll die tryin…"

Hugh struggled to his feet but his left leg crumpled beneath him. He fell to his knees. He tried again but he couldn't put weight on that left leg, let alone walk on it. "Well, if'n I can't walk, I'll have to crawl," Hugh muttered.

He pulled the bearskin over his shoulders. The skin would protect him from cold and weather and provide a bed to sleep on. Dragging his left leg, on hands and one knee, Hugh, looking more bear than man, crawled into the night.

Hugh begins his crawl

"You will live in constant suspense, filled with dread both night and day, never sure of your life."
Deuteronomy 28:66

THE CRAWL

That first night Hugh probably covered less than a mile. As dawn broke, he spread the bearskin in the hollow of a creek bed, and fell into a fitful sleep. He dreamed that he'd reached a river and was floating on a raft toward Ft. Kiowa.

When he awoke, the moon was high overhead. Hugh stretched his stiff body and reached into his pocket for more berries. Pulling the bearskin over his shoulders, he slowly crawled southeast following the creek bottom.

Fighting thirst and hunger, Hugh inched his way across the prairie. An occasional thunderstorm provided a fresh drink of water. Mostly Hugh drank from sinkholes or buffalo wallows. His years spent with the Pawnees had taught him to dig a root called breadfruit when there was nothing else to eat. The root stopped the rumbling in his stomach but he needed meat to keep going. Ground squirrels and prairie dogs scampered just beyond his reach. Sometimes he imagined how he'd use a loop of string placed around their hole to catch a gopher. Finally, Hugh came upon a snake. Using a large rock, he killed it and ate the raw meat. Even though it was hard to chew and swallow, he forced it down. Feeling stronger, Hugh kept going.

Hugh lost count of the nights he crawled. As each sunrise glimmered in the eastern sky, he rolled up in the bearskin to sleep. The sun was sinking in the west each night when he'd roll off the bearskin to continue the crawl. Always hungry, always looking for a drink, he crawled.

Anger burned inside him as he crawled. Anger kept him crawling when he wanted to give up.

The prairie stretched out ahead of him. He watched a tall butte in the far distance slowly grow closer and closer to him as he crawled. At last, he reached the base of Thunder Butte. He rested there. The next night he crawled on with the butte now fading behind him.

After many nights of slow progress, Hugh was worn out and discouraged. He had only berries to eat since killing the snake. His body again needed meat to keep him going.

Dawn was breaking when he spotted a pack of wolves in the growing light of day. They were tearing at the carcass of a buffalo calf. Hugh hungrily waited for the wolves to eat their fill. Then he lumbered toward them, growling. In the early morning light, Hugh looked very much like a grizzly. The wolves retreated. As Hugh feasted on what was left of the buffalo calf, the pack watched from a distance. With his hunger finally satisfied, Hugh stuffed bits of raw meat into his pockets. He needed to put some distance between him and the wolves, so Hugh crawled all day and into the night. Guiding him on were the stars that had become his nightly companions.

Glass frightens wolves away from a buffalo calf

After many long nights of following creek bottoms, he finally reached the banks of the Moreau River. Hugh crawled into the waters. He was thankful for a drink but bitterly disappointed. The river was too shallow for a raft. Discouraged, Hugh rolled out his bearskin not far from the river. As the sun began to rise over the prairie, Hugh fell asleep.

"When you pass through the rivers, they will not sweep over you." Isaiah 43:2

RESCUED!

One night Hugh came upon a deserted Arikara village. Digging through the ashes of a campfire, he found the blade of a knife. He needed a tool to make a crutch. With a crutch, he could travel faster. Nights were getting colder. He must reach Ft. Kiowa before winter storms descended on the prairie.

In a creek bottom, Hugh spotted a tree with a low hanging branch. The Y formed by its branches was perfect for a crutch. Hugh whittled with the blade. Finally, he was able to free the branch. Using his new crutch, he pulled himself slowly to his feet. He felt like a man again. He could walk!

Geese honked as they flew overhead on their way south. Hugh gazed longingly at them, wishing he could take wing and fly with them. Leaves on the bushes in the creek bottoms turned golden.

The bearskin was heavy and harder to carry now that he walked with the crutch. Many times Hugh considered leaving it behind. But, he had no way of making a fire to keep warm. In case an early winter storm hit, he'd need the skin to protect him from the weather.

Early one fall morning, Hugh came to the top of a high bluff. Tired from a night of travel, he was eager to find a place to rest for a few hours. He began to pick his way carefully down the rough bank. In the breaking light of a new day, he saw a bright shimmer. A river was winding below him…a large river….finally! His chances of surviving were now very real. He could make a raft of driftwood large enough to carry him, and float downriver to Ft. Kiowa. Forgetting how tired he was and how dangerous it was to travel in daylight, he headed for the wooded river bottom of the Cheyenne River.

Movement in the trees brought him to a stop. Hugh saw ten or twelve mounted Indians slowly winding their way along the banks of the river. Fear froze him in his tracks. Had he come so far only to die at the hands of the Rees? Hugh's hope of survival seemed to be drifting away as swiftly as the rushing waters of the river.

Could he run fast enough to escape? He knew the approaching Indians would overtake him quickly on their horses. His years with the Pawnees reminded him to be brave. He drew the bear hide more tightly around him as if it were protection and waited.

Discovered by the Lakota

The braves stopped a short distance from Hugh. Hugh's face broke into a welcoming grin when he realized they were friendly Lakota. He raised his hand in greeting.

Puzzled, they looked at the figure before them. What was this? A bear with the face of a white man? Hugh motioned the Indians to come closer. They slid from their ponies and slowly walked toward Hugh.

Using sign language, Hugh told this story... how he had traveled to the land of the Rees. There he fought and killed the mighty Bear. He showed them the scars on his back and face. White men took his weapons and left him to die alone. Picking up a twig, he drew in the sand, showing the forked river far to the north. He showed the Lakota how he had crawled from there for many moons finally arriving in their land. Hugh asked if they would help him to get back to his own people. Hugh knew the Pawnees believed that the Great Spirit blessed anyone who survived a bear attack. That person was treated with special respect. His hope was that the Lakota too would believe they would be blessed by helping White Bear Man. They spoke quietly to each other and then nodded. Hugh was thankful he'd decided not to run.

Helping Hugh onto one of their ponies, they headed downstream to their village. That night, for the first time since the attack, he slept undisturbed by dreams.

The next morning Hugh awoke to the sounds and smells of breakfast being prepared. The Lakota stew and fry bread seemed more delicious than anything he had ever eaten.

With rest and food, Hugh's strength returned. His leg healed and he could walk without the crutch. The Lakota agreed to give their new friend, White Bear Man, one of their ponies. After a few days of rest, Hugh headed for Ft. Kiowa. As he rode out of the Lakota camp, Hugh knew these prairie dwellers had saved his life.

Ft. Kiowa near the Missouri River

"Act with courage, and may the LORD be with those who do well." II Chronicles 19:11

FT. KIOWA AT LAST

The news that Hugh Glass had died on the banks of the Grand had already spread through the territory. So when this tall, thin, scarred man on an Indian pony arrived at Ft. Kiowa in late November and announced he was Hugh Glass, it took awhile before anyone believed him. The soldiers listened spellbound as he told of being left to die, how he'd crawled from the Grand River to the Cheyenne River where the Lakota rescued him.

Glass was strong again. And he was angry as a wounded grizzly. Getting even with Fitzgerald and Jim burned in his heart. He stayed at the fort only long enough to gather supplies and information. When Hugh learned Fitz was no longer with the mountain men but had joined the army, he was easy to find.

Fitz nearly died of fright the day Hugh caught up with him. Hugh grabbed him by the throat. Fitz was sure a ghost had been sent to haunt him for leaving Hugh to die. He begged for mercy. When Hugh demanded the return of Ole Faithful, a stunned Fitz realized this was no ghost and he gladly returned the rifle. Hugh had to be content with giving him a good scare. Shooting a soldier would mean jail or maybe even death by a firing squad. With Ole Faithful on his shoulder, Hugh left Fitz, shaken, but thankful to be alive.

By the time Hugh found Jim, having Ole Faithful back had eased his anger. He gave Jim a real tongue-lashing on what a no-good friend he'd been. Jim begged for forgiveness. He told Hugh he'd had not a moment of peace since leaving him there to die. Jim said he would spend the rest of his life making it up to the Old Man. For a long time Hugh looked deep into Jim's eyes. Without a word, he got back on his pony and rode away. Losing Hugh again was harder on Jim then any beating. His eyes filled with tears as his old friend, without a backward look, left him. Jim couldn't see that Hugh was crying too.

Hugh and Ole Faithful continued to roam the plains of the west.

Several years later, Hugh met up once again with his old enemy, the Rees. This time he didn't escape. His life ended there on a stretch of frozen river.

Hugh Glass, prairie adventurer and survivor, lives on in the books written about him and in the minds and imaginations of those who read his story.

HISTORICAL FOOTNOTES

John Neihardt, poet laureate, and author of "The Song of Hugh Glass", was among a group of individuals who placed a marker in 1923 near the forks of the Grand River at the site of the attack. That early marker told of the amazing courage displayed by Hugh Glass. The construction of a dam near Shadehill in the 60s has made access to this monument impossible. In 1939, Neihardt was invited to Bison to help dedicate the new school and a Hugh Glass monument in the parking lot. Neihardt's words that day encouraged the people of Perkins County to carry on the courageous spirit that Hugh Glass displayed on his crawl. The monument in Bison tells of the route Glass probably followed. He crawled only a few miles to the west of Meadow where I grew up. In 1964, a new monument was erected on a bank above Shadehill Dam. A few years later, John Neihardt visited the Bison School. I was teaching in the school system at the time and was impressed by this elderly man and his stories of the past. Neihardt, through his writings, hoped to preserve the memory of Hugh Glass and his courageous crawl.

Beginning his crawl near the Grand River, Hugh Glass crawled southeast crossing the Moreau River and contined on toward the Cheyenne River. He finally arrived at Fort Kiowa. Now underwater, that fort was near present day Oacoma. As the crow flies, he traveled a distance of nearly 200 miles.

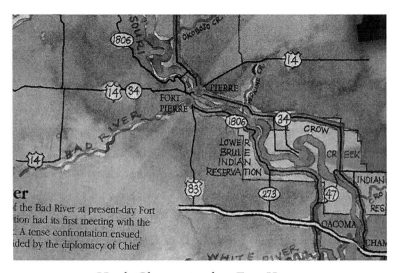

Hugh Glass arrived at Fort Kiowa.
Now underwater, that fort was near present day
Oacoma. As the crow flies, he traveled a
distance of almost 200 miles.

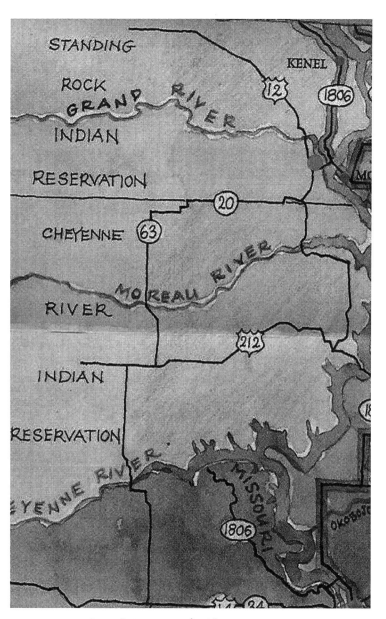

Grand, Moreau & Cheyenne Rivers

Author Margie La Due with two former students,
Roy Goddard and Britnee Aaker.

ABOUT THE AUTHOR

Margaret (Margie) LaDue grew up in Meadow, SD during the 1940s and 50s. She graduated Bison High School, married and graduated Black Hills State College with a degree in Elementary Education during the 60s. She and husband, Gary, lived in Florida and California while he served in the navy during the Vietnam War. They eventually settled on Gary's South Dakota family farm where they raised a son and two daughters while teaching and ranching. After retiring from a 33 year career in teaching, Margie enjoys traveling and spending time with her four grandsons, ages 5, 3, and 2 and a newborn.

ABOUT THE ILLUSTRATOR

Anne Ellingson, one of the author's many second graders, grew up about ten miles southwest of the forks of the Grand River. She is a country girl who enjoys history. Anne graduated Bison High School, Bison, South Dakota in 2005. She spent several months studying art at Salt Lake Community College in Salt Lake City, Utah. Anne hopes to pursue art as a career.

"Show me your ways, O LORD, teach me your
paths; guide me in your truth…
My hope is in you all day long."
Psalm 25: 4, 5

REFLECTIONS OF
A FIRST TIME AUTHOR

During the years I taught elementary school, I shared with each class the story of Hugh Glass. The children listened intently and were eager to know more about him. So we left the classroom to walk to the monument that stands on the school parking lot. Together we read the words inscribed there:

In Memory of Hugh Glass
Hunter with Ashley's fur traders,
mauled by a grizzly bear while
camping at the forks of Grand River

north of Bison in 1823. Left for dead,
he survived, crawled south between
the present towns of Bison and Meadow,
hiding from Indians by day, to
Ft. Kiowa 150 miles away.
Dr. John Neihardt tells the tale in
"The Song of Hugh Glass".

Conner Palmer and Dani Kling
by the Bison Hugh Glass Monument